Sophie's Bucket

BY CATHERINE STOCK

A VOYAGER BOOK
HARCOURT BRACE & COMPANY
San Diego   New York   London

Requests for permission to make copies
of any part of the work should be mailed to:
Permissions Department,
Harcourt Brace & Company, 8th Floor,
Orlando, Florida 32887.

Library of Congress Cataloging-in-Publication Data
available upon request.
ISBN 0-15-277162-X (pbk.)

A B C D E (pbk.)

Printed in Singapore

For Patrick

Sophie woke up one morning to find two green and blue packages at the bottom of her bed.

In the first one was a new
striped bathing suit. In the
second one was a bucket—a
bright yellow bucket with pale
blue stars.

Her father looked into the room.

"We're going to the seashore next week," he said.

"Wow!" Sophie could hardly wait.

Finally Saturday arrived, and they all got into the car. Sophie put her bear in the bucket and held them both in her lap.

All the way there, Sophie asked questions. She had never seen the sea.

"What is the bucket for?"

"To put things in," said her mother.

"Can I put the sea in my bucket?" asked Sophie.

"Some of the sea," said her father.

On Sunday, Sophie woke up in a different bed, in a different room, in a different house! But there were her bear and the bucket.

"We're at the sea!" Sophie jumped out of bed.

Her mother made a tuna fish sandwich and put it in the bucket with an orange for Sophie's lunch. "Let's go, Sophie," she called.

The sun was bright and the sky was blue and the sea stretched out forever. Sophie felt so small!

They dropped their towels and raced down the beach. Her mother and father lifted her high as they jumped over the waves.

The water was cold. But the sun was hot. Sophie put her bucket in the sea. Then she put some sea in her bucket. She splashed the water on her mother's toes.

"Too late. I'm wet already!" Her mother laughed.

"Can I put the sand in my bucket?" asked Sophie.

"Some of it," said her father, and he helped her build a sand castle.

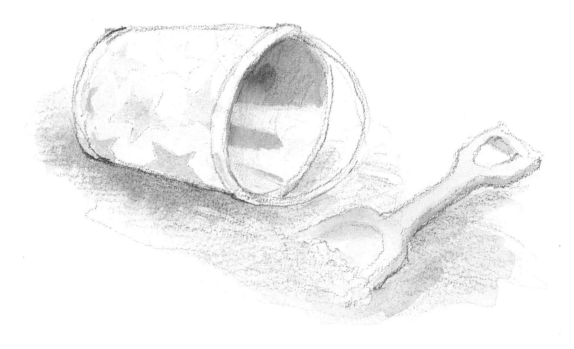

"What else can we put in the bucket?" asked Sophie.

"We can collect some shells," said her mother. They even found a starfish.

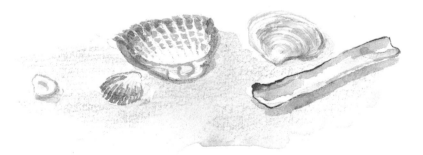

"Sophie, come and see what's hiding under your bucket," her father called.

Sophie lifted the bucket carefully and watched a little pink crab scuttle back into the water.

That evening they watched the
sun sink into the sea, and the
moon rise.

They made a fire and roasted
sausages on long sticks.

It was time to go home. Her mother packed up the basket and her father folded up their blanket.

Sophie put her special new treasures into the bucket: some sand, some water, some shells, some seaweed, and the starfish.

"Look," whispered Sophie.

There was the moon, glowing softly in the bucket.

"The moon must want to come with us too," said her father.
And he picked up Sophie and the bucket with the sand and the water and the shells and the seaweed and the starfish and the moon and carried them all home.